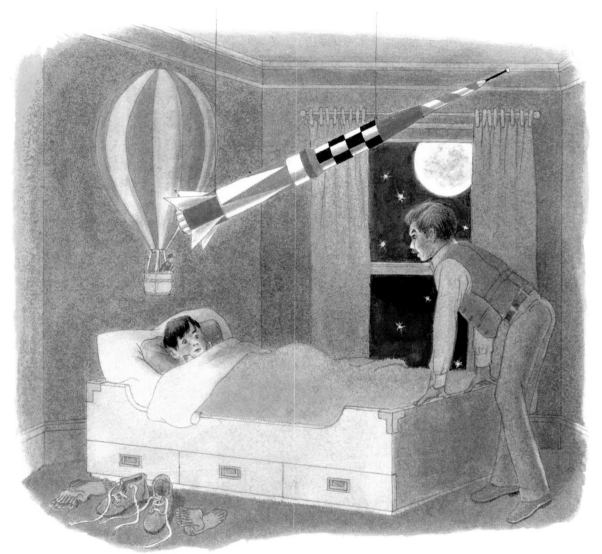

THE·PLANET·OF·LOST·THINGS

The Planet of Lost Things

STORY · BY · MARK · STRAND

ILLUSTRATIONS · BY · WILLIAM · PÈNE · DU BOIS

Clarkson N. Potter, Inc. / Publishers / NEW YORK DISTRIBUTED BY CROWN PUBLISHERS, INC.

Luke's father had told him a story, but Luke was not tired and wanted to hear another. His father said, "It's too late to start a new story, but here's a question you can think about until you go to sleep: If a tree falls in a forest and no one is there to hear it fall, does it make a sound?"

Luke's father left the room, and the moon shone down from the black star-filled sky and its light fell upon Luke like the finest white powder.

Luke dreamed he was an astronaut dressed in a silver suit. He dreamed he leaped from his bedroom window in one slow bound to the launching pad where a spaceship waited.

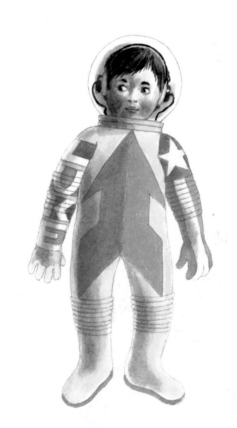

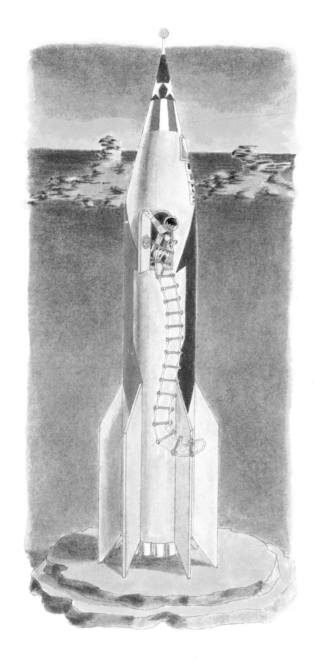

He got in and, as if he had always known how, he pushed the right buttons and the spaceship lifted off.

Luke knew The Solar System by heart and named each of the planets as he flew by them.

Mercury.

Venus.

Mars.

Jupiter.

He took a turn around Saturn but decided against going on to Neptune, Uranus, and Pluto, which were too far away. As he headed toward Earth, Luke said to himself, "I certainly know my way around." But on his way back, Luke noticed a planet he did not know the name of. He decided to investigate.

The moment he stepped out of his spaceship he heard a tremendous sound, the sound of a tree falling in a forest. But he saw no forest, not a single tree. "This," said Luke to himself, "must be the place where all the sound that was never heard goes."

Luke had not gone very far from the spaceship when he noticed a building with columns in front.

When he peeked inside, he saw bundles of letters and packages neatly stacked. No one was there. "These must be things that got lost in the mail," Luke thought.

The stillness frightened him. He left in a hurry.

As he walked on, he saw more things he recognized collected into neat piles.

He saw socks, mittens, combs, and hats. He saw needles that had been lost in haystacks. He saw keys that had fallen from the purses of women running for buses. He saw money that had fallen from pockets. He even saw tissues neatly piled that had been lost flying out of automobiles traveling very fast across the desert.

When Luke had walked for a while, he saw an iron fenced-in place with dogs and cats inside. "They must have been lost," he said to himself, and he tried to pet one of them.

He saw several huge clouds of balloons that were higher than the tallest buildings on Earth and as big around as a whole city block.

"I am sure some of the balloons I've lost are in these giant piles," Luke thought. He was about to pick out a balloon when two people appeared. One was a woman carrying a small suitcase and the other was a soldier in uniform.

"Hello," said Luke.

"Hello," said the woman and the soldier.

"Nice day," said Luke.

"So so," said the soldier.

"Can you tell me where I am, please?" asked Luke.

"We don't really know," said the woman. "This planet has never been discovered. As soon as it's found, it's lost again. And as soon as it's named, its name is forgotten."

"And who are you?" asked Luke.

"I'm a missing person," said the woman. And pointing to her suitcase, she said, "These are my clothes that are missing, too."

"Have a balloon," said The Missing Person.

"I am The Unknown Soldier," said the soldier. "Actually, I am just one of them. There are quite a few, you know."

"And who are you?" they asked.

"Hmmm, I can't remember," said Luke, "and I can't remember what I was looking for either."

"That's par for the course up here," said The Unknown Soldier. "No one is supposed to remember."

"Wait! I do remember something," said Luke. "I came on a spaceship."

"Where is it?" asked The Missing Person.

"I can't remember," said Luke. "But maybe we can retrace my steps."

"Impossible," said The Unknown Soldier. "Up here all tracks vanish; the wind erases all footprints."

"Oh, come now," said The Missing Person, "if we walk around a bit, I'm sure we'll find it."

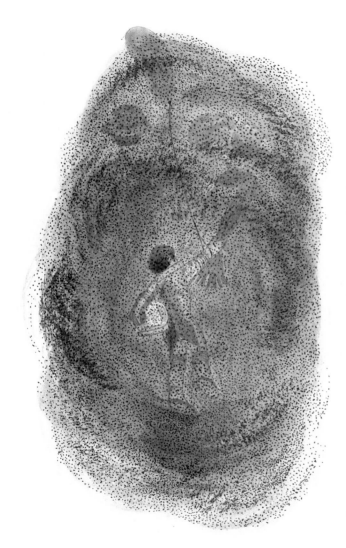

So the three started walking without any idea of where they were going. But suddenly the air became gray and sooty, and they could not see one another. They had to yell to stay in contact.

"I bet you're worried, little boy," said The Missing Person. "No need to be. We'll get out of this mess."

"It's a mess, all right," said The Unknown Soldier. "Smoke from factories! Dust shaken from mops! Pretty soon there won't be any fresh air left."

"You worry too much," said The Missing Person.

At that moment Luke heard a moaning, whistling wind at his back.

"Here's that poor wind again!" yelled The Missing Person. "It does nothing but circle the planet."

"Where does it come from?" asked Luke.

"Oh, it's just air that was let out of tires and now keeps looking for new tires to get back into," said The Missing Person. "See? It's blowing away the smoke and dust."

The round clouds of sooty air had been pushed away by the wind, and Luke was able to see his companions again. The Unknown Soldier was standing at attention, and The Missing Person was sitting on her suitcase, filing her nails.

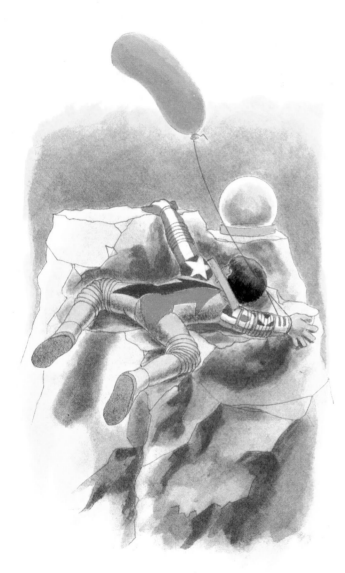

"Well, now what?" said The Missing Person.

"I think we should climb that mountain," said The Unknown Soldier, pointing straight ahead. "From up there I am sure we'll spot the spaceship."

So they climbed the mountain, and when they got to the top, they had a wonderful view of the planet. In the distance, not far from The Building of Lost Letters and Packages, they saw the spaceship.

"Let's hurry," said Luke, wanting to get to it before dark.

"Don't fall," said The Missing Person, who was having trouble carrying her suitcase down the steep incline.

When they got to the foot of the mountain, two friendly auks came up to Luke. Behind them, at the far end of the horizon, hung a great curtain of mist.

"The auks come from the plain where mist that has risen from rivers early in the morning is collected," said The Unknown Soldier. "That is where the extinct animals live. They roam and howl and never stop. Look! You can see them through that break in the mist! Too bad we can't pay them a visit—they are dangerous and, besides, it's out of our way."

"Easy come, easy go," said The Missing Person. "We'll pass an even better place that's right on our route."

"What is it?" asked Luke.

"You'll see," said The Missing Person.

And off they went, The Unknown Soldier leading the way.

They passed a place where the ground seemed strewn with diamonds.

"Is that the place?" asked Luke.

"No," said The Unknown Soldier, "that is only the dew that goes away when the sun comes up."

Finally, they arrived at the place The Missing Person had mentioned. And there Luke saw rabbits, glasses of water, and colorful scarves.

"Wow!" said Luke. "What's all this?"

"This is where everything goes that magicians make disappear," said The Missing Person.

Arriving at the spaceship, Luke's companions said good-bye to him and made him promise never to remember what had happened on his visit. But as soon as Luke put his foot on the ladder to the cockpit, he suddenly remembered his name. "I'm Luke," he yelled.

"We'll forget," they yelled back, waving.

The lift-off was perfect, and soon Luke was on his way back to Earth, steering with one hand and holding his balloon with the other.

When he landed, he ran straight to his house. He was back in bed and asleep before the sun rose.

When Luke's mother came in to wake him for breakfast, she saw him sound asleep with his arm in the air. And she said, "Luke dear, are you holding a balloon?"

Half-asleep, Luke said that he thought he'd held one all night.

"Then where is it, Sweetheart?"

"I càn't remember," Luke said.

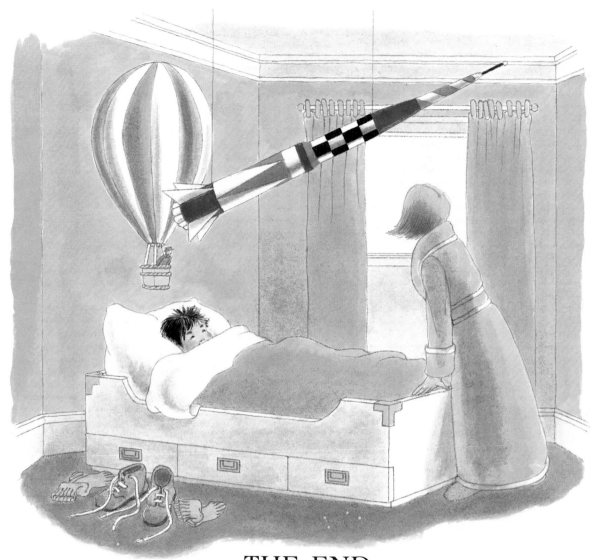

THE END

Published by Clarkson N. Potter, Inc., One Park
Avenue, New York, New York 10016
and published simultaneously in Canada by
General Publishing Company Limited.

Printed in Hong Kong by South China Printing Co.

Library of Congress Cataloging in Publication Data

Strand, Mark, 1934–
The planet of lost things.

Summary: Luke meets a Missing Person and an Unknown
Soldier on the planet where lost things are found.
[1. Fantasy. 2. Lost and found possessions—Fiction]
I. DuBois, William Pène, 1916–   ill. II. Title.
PZ7.S8967P 1982   [Fic]   81-19138
ISBN: 0-517-54184X   AACR2

Design by Carl Barile

10 9 8 7 6 5 4 3 2 1

First Edition